Tomie de Paola's KITTEN KIDS™ and the Big Camp-out

A GOLDEN BOOK · NEW YORK
Western Publishing Company, Inc., Racine, Wisconsin 53404

 Produced by The Philip Lief Group, Inc. Illustrated by D&R Animation. Printed in the U.S.A. Library of Congress Catalog Card Number: 87-81925 ISBN: 0-307-10612-8/ISBN: 0-307-60612-0 (lib. bdg.)
A B C D E F G H I J K L M

"Look, Kit!" Katie said, holding up the mail. "It's a postcard from Cousin Tom! It says he is coming to see us tomorrow!"

"Oh, goody," said Kit, clapping his hands. He and Katie loved it when their cousin Tom came to visit. Tom was big. He was two years older than Katie. He and his family lived in the city, far away.

Whenever Cousin Tom came, Katie and Kit were allowed to do wonderful things.

"Maybe Tom will take us to the playground at the Park School again," said Kit. "That was really fun."

"Or all the way over to the old train station," said Katie happily.

They went outside and sat on the front steps.

"We must plan something extra special," said Katie, "so Tom will be glad he came."

"Something that's as much fun as the circus and the zoo and the museum with the dinosaurs!" said Kit.

"Something that Tom can't do in the city!" Katie said.

They thought and thought. Suddenly Kit jumped up. "I know what we can do!" he said. And he ran into the house.

In a few minutes Kit came back. He was carrying the new tent Grandma and Grandpa had given them so they could sleep outside in their own backyard.

"Tom can't sleep outside in the city," Kit said.

"You're right!" said Katie. "Let's ask Mama and Papa if it's okay."

Mama and Papa said yes.
"You may use this flashlight," said Papa.
"And you can borrow this portable radio," Mama said.

Katie and Kit spent the whole next day getting ready. They set up the tent. They packed cookies and marshmallows and apples to eat for snacks. And Kit brought out some of his favorite picture books.

They had just finished when the doorbell rang. It was Tom!

"Hi, Cousins," he said.

Katie and Kit could hardly wait to show Tom the tent.
"Pretty neat!" Tom said.

After dinner they hurried outside to begin their adventure. It was still light enough for them to play ball in the yard and climb in the trees.

As the sun began to set they caught lightning bugs in jars with little holes punched in the tops.

Finally it was time to crawl into the tent for the night.

"Let's tell stories," said Kit. He was hoping that Tom or Katie would read to him from one of his picture books.

"Sure!" said Tom. "But not those baby stories. I'll make up something real, real scary."

"Well, okay—I guess," said Katie slowly. She was a little afraid to hear a scary story, but she didn't want Tom to know it.

Kit felt like saying no, but he didn't want Tom to think he was a baby. So he didn't say anything.

Then Tom began. "Once upon a time there was a ghost." He made his voice sound spooky. "It wasn't an ordinary ghost. It was the ghost of a pirate! And at the end of his arm there was a hook instead of a hand!"

Suddenly a curved shadow appeared on the side of the tent. Tom stopped talking and gave a yowl.

"What—what's that hooklike thing I see through the tent?" Tom asked, sounding frightened.

Cautiously Katie peeked outside the tent. "Oh, I see," she said. "It's just a shadow from one of the trees. Did it scare you?"

"Uh, no," said Tom. "Uh, I was just pretending."

"Well, it didn't scare me," said Katie.

Kit snuggled closer to Katie. He had been very scared.

Tom bent his hand like a hook and continued the story. "The ghost of the pirate was looking for someone. Can you guess who?"

"WHOOOOOOO" they heard from outside the tent.

Tom's eyes became as big as saucers. "It's the ghost!" he whispered.

Kit laughed out loud. This time he wasn't scared. "It's just an owl, Tom," he said. "We hear them all the time around here."

"I knew that," said Tom. But his eyes were still as big as saucers.

In a big voice Tom went on with the story. "The ghost was trying to find—" Suddenly there was a loud crash. Katie and Kit both jumped, and Tom scrambled to his feet.

"That wasn't a shadow, and that wasn't an owl either!" Tom shrieked.

All three of them raced from the tent.

They ran toward the house. They ran past the overturned garbage can and the raccoon family that was searching though the scraps for its dinner. They stopped running.

"Look," said Kit. "It was only some hungry raccoons."

"I'll bet you two were really scared," said Tom. He smiled weakly.

"I'll bet you're right!" said Kit.

Katie looked at both of them. "You know what?" she said. "I have a great idea." And she whispered her idea first to Tom and then to Kit.

So Tom was able to finish his story without any more interruptions.

"Ever since the ship went down, the ghost of the pirate has roamed the earth, looking for a place to rest!" he said.

"That was a really scary story, Tom," said Kit.

"And that was a really great idea about the tent, Katie," said Tom.

Then the three cousins said good night and fell asleep in the special tent Grandma and Grandpa had given to Katie and Kit.

Good night, Kitten Kids. Good night, Cousin Tom.